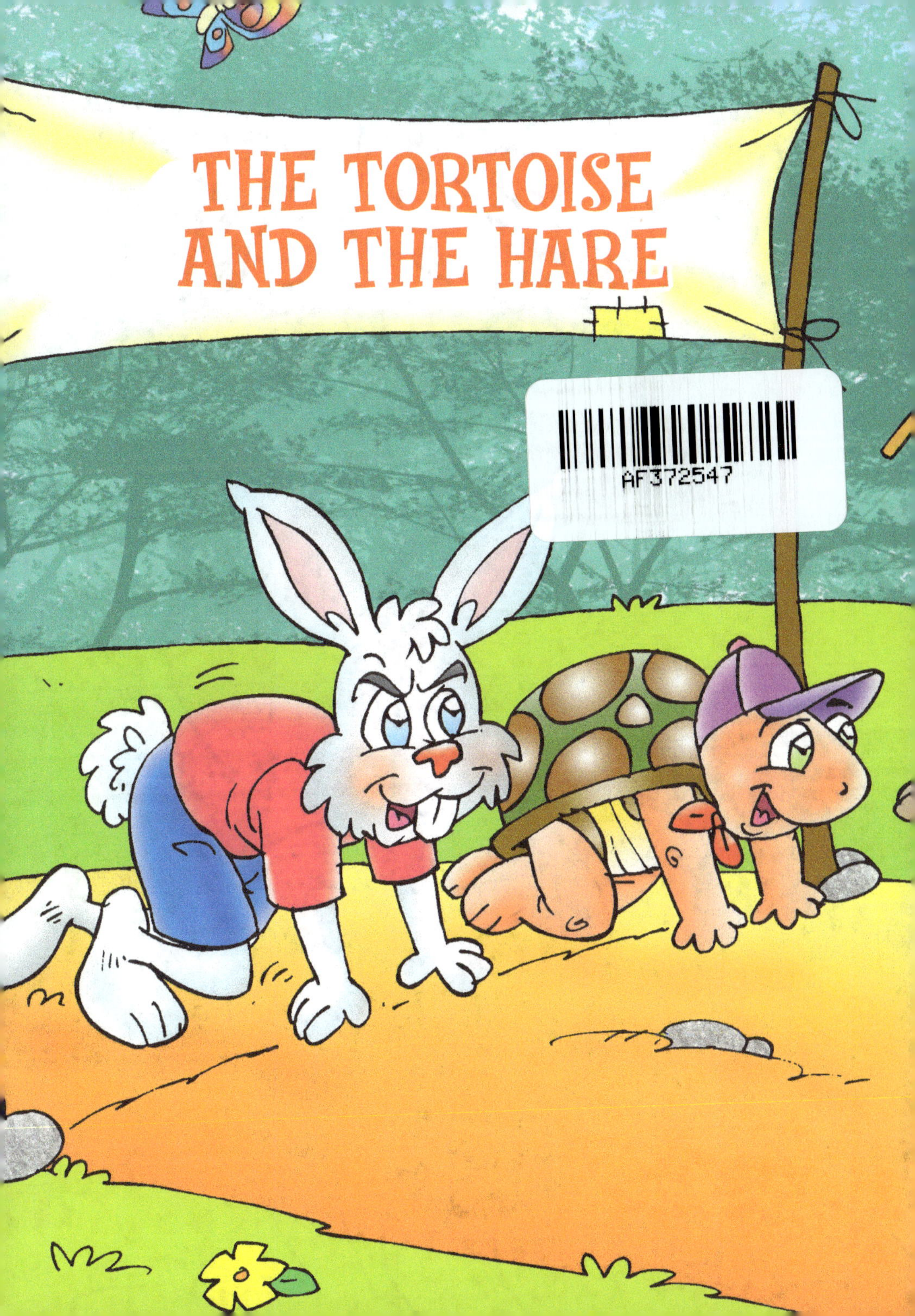

THE TORTOISE
AND THE HARE
AF372547

ONCE UPON A TIME, THERE WAS A HARE THAT ALWAYS WANDERED THROUGH THE FOREST.

BEING VERY FAST, THE HARE LOVED TO
TAUNT THE TORTOISE, SAYING THAT SHE WAS
THE SLOWEST ANIMAL OF ALL.

ONE DAY, TIRED OF THE HARE'S TAUNTS, THE TORTOISE CHALLEGENGED HER TO A RACE.

THE HARE LAUGHED AT THE TORTOISE,
AS SHE KNEW THERE WAS NO CHANCE OF
LOSING TO HER OPPONENT.

THE NEXT DAY, THE HARE AND THE TORTOISE ARRIVED AT THE FOREST FOR THEIR RACE.
START

THEY POSITIONED THEMSELVES AT
THE STARTING POINT AND, AFTER THE
COUNTDOWN, RACED OFF.

IN A FEW MOMENTS, THE HARE WAS
FAR AHEAD.

BUT THE TORTOISE, ALWAYS PERSISTENT,
CONTINUED TO RUN AS FAST AS SHE COULD.

START

WHEN SHE LOOKED BACK AND SAW THAT HER OPPONENT WAS PRACTICALLY IN THE SAME PLACE...

...THE HARE DECIDED TO STOP UNDER A TREE
TO EAT AND REST.

AFTER DEVOURING SEVERAL CARROTS, THE HARE BECAME VERY SLEEPY AND ENDED UP FALLING INTO A DEEP SLEEP.
ZZZZZZ

SUDDENLY, WITHOUT HER NOTICING,
THE TORTOISE OVERTOOK HER.

WHEN SHE FINALLY WOKE UP, THE HARE SAW
THAT THE TORTOISE WAS JUST A FEW STEPS
FROM THE FINISH LINE.

FINISH

SHE RAN AS FAST AS SHE COULD IN AN ATTEMPT TO WIN THE RACE, BUT SHE COULDN'T CATCH UP TO HER OPPONENT.

THE TORTOISE THEN SHOWED THE HARE THAT IT'S NOT ENOUGH TO JUST BE THE FASTEST, BUT IT'S ALSO NECESSARY TO HAVE DETERMINATION AND PERSISTENCE.

SO, THE HARE LEARNED THE LESSON AND
STARTED TO RESPECT THE DIFFERENCES AND
CHARACTERISTICS OF EACH ANIMAL.

THE END.